The Tiny Tale

Assemblage of four genres of Scribbling

THE TINY TALE

Naaz Nayim

Presented by
Peaceful Writers International

ACKNOWLEDGEMENT

First and foremost, I would like to thank the almighty for the rendering me life and talent to scribble.
A warm acknowledgement and tonnes of love to my father and my mother for supporting me throughout and for believing in me and loving the passion I have decided to pursue.
I would like to extend my heartiest acknowledgement to my friends and loved ones for encouraging and boosting me up every time I thought of giving up writing.
It would be injustice if I don't mention them. Monalisa for always guiding me through the correct track.Udit for motivating me every time and praising whatever I wrote. Jagriti for all her emotional support and consistent help to focuss on writing. Archishman for getting this masterpiece published with all ease and always hitting me to write a better one. Nausheen for always cheering me up to write more. Riya, for managing everything so well. And, Vivek for always being there as my back support during toughest of times.
I thank every single soul who helped us to bring this dream book of mine, a successful one.
I thank Peaceful Writers International Publishing house team for providing this wonderful platform.

Dedicated to all my Readers
&
Well Wishers!

GENRE:
ACROSTIC POETRY

CONTENTS

<u>COLOURS</u>

Canvas of different emotions

Offering several melancholies and ecstasies.

Loving the deepest scars

Others pulling us down

Utmost care we deserve to bruish ourselves.

Rusting memories killing us

Sacrificing everything we loved.

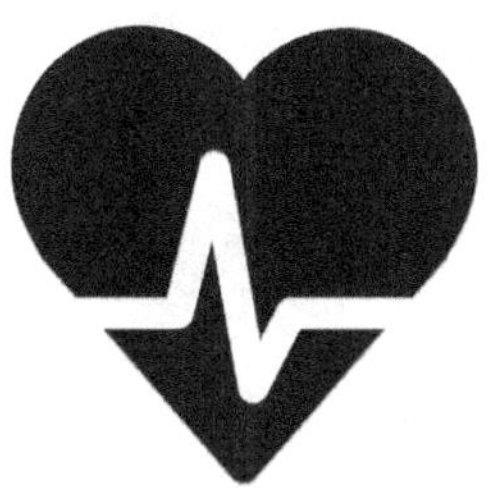

LIFE

Luring us to the worst paths
Inking out my fear for everything
Facing challenges with pride and confidence
Eagerly waiting to get healed with love.

<u>DEPRESSION</u>

Down the lane,

Expressing Fear ain't easy.

Paranormal conscience hitting hard,

Pulchritudinously exploiting us.

Relief becomes a dream,

Expecting reality is difficult.

Somberness is lost.

Sleeps becomes extinct.

Imagination skills weakens.

Out of the context world seems.

Never judge a depressed person.

IMAGINATION

I found myself in a deserted land,
Maybe deep into myself lies some melancholies,
Amidst the peace I could sense noises,
Glittered past has went into vain,
Inside capturing the pain,
Not letting me to live as myself,
Alluring me to sadness,
Tired heart beating just for the sake to beat,
Imagine letting the world sleep,
On the seashore,
Navigating happiness.

FRIEND

Fading memories they repaint it.

Renders a helping hand.

Imagining loneliness with them is myth

Euphoria they possess.

Never they pull you down.

Draps a sheet of protection.

# WRITER

Wearies is not in their perception.

Ready to shine with their imagination.

Insane to scribble.

Thoughts wander in every ambience.

Ecstasy they find in inking,

Raining emotions and truths they portray.

<u>ECOSYSTEM</u>

Exemplifies there's no life without proper care.
Condones all the cruelty showered upon them.
Obnoxious they feel but the fact is concealed.
Sardonic behaviour of humans they tolerate.
Yowl of the nature is suppressed cruelty.
Sagacious behavior they expect.
Temperamental behaviour is creating pain.
Ebullient ambience has vanished somewhere.
Magnanimous creatures as also cutting deep.

<u>POEM</u>

Personalised thoughts of fiction.

Origin of uniqueness.

Ecstasy and expressive in tiny verses.

Memories penned down in ease.

LONELY

Lonesome isolated with inner tenebrosity.

Obfuscation feelings they deal with.

Never ready to give up easily.

Eager to fight all the cold wars.

Lonely yet powerful.

Yonder in confused blacks.

RAPE

Regret runs in blood,

Astonished for years by the incident.

Pressurised to keep it a secret.

Easy is not to survive.

GENRE:
ELCHEN POETRY

CONTENT

<u>LAKE</u>

Lake,
Reflecting Sunlight,
Flows with emotions,
Soothes the bruise heart,
Splintered.

<u>WINDS</u>

Winds,
Blowing Around,
Amidst the chaos,
Cools down the vehemence,
Ameliorating.

<u>TREE</u>

Tree,
Standing Tall,
Portraying the strength,
Pain that they bear
Smiling.

<u>BIRDS</u>

Birds,
Chirping Around,
Ecstasy they vibe,
Melody singing for us,
Peacefully.

<u>ANIMALS</u>

Animals,
Loitering Around,
Wandering for shelter,
Pain and beatings they,
Suffer.

<u>**FLOWERS**</u>

Flowers,
Blooming beauty,
Smell of heaven,
Freshening the mind of,
Humans.

<u>FRUITS</u>

Fruits,
Producing nature,
Feeding every individual,
Providing a shielded life,
Successfully.

MOON

Moon,
Nights glory,
Symbol of affection,
Bounding two loved souls,
Sacredly.

<u>STARS</u>

Stars,
Sparkling beauty,
Symbolising past memories,
Reminder of presence in,
Life.

<u>GRASS</u>

Grass,
Possessing greenery,
Portraying perennial behaviour,
Rooted with immense strength,
Proudly.

<u>SOIL</u>

Soil,
Binding life,
Decaying with time,
Supporting humanhood to stand,
United.

<u>WATER</u>

Water,
Flowing selflessly,
Cleaning necessary dirts,
Absorbing all the pains,
Quietly.

<u>SKY</u>

Sky,
Exploring galaxy,
Beautifying the universe,
Limits of every person,
Dreaming.

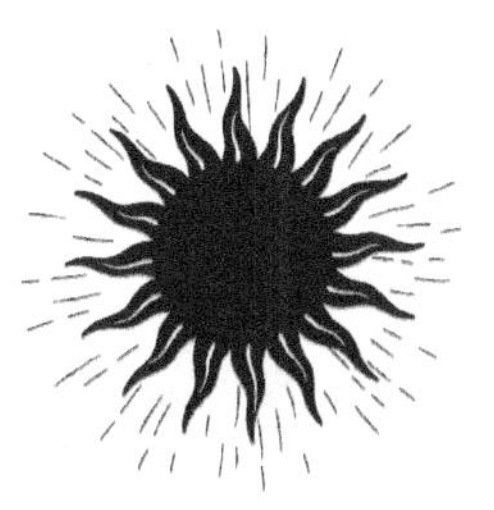

SUNLIGHT

Sunlight,
Helping Hand,
Providing appropriate nutrition,
To the source provider,
Plant.

FIRE

Fire,
Distressed misery,
Concealing anger blast,
Blasts with immense injury,
Unhealed.

<u>ADULT</u>

Adult,
Ruined self,
Depression running along,
Skeleton struggling with miserable,
Conditions.

CHILDREN

Children,
Crying soul,
Bearing child labour,
Facing the cruel world,
Unwillingly.

TRANSGENDER

Transgender,
Idiosyncratic creature,
Curse of God,
Adjusting in the world,
Weeping.

THUNDER

Thunder,
Crackles life,
Horrifies the evils,
Shakens the broken thread,
Entangled.

MONUMENT

Monuments,
Standing strong,
Signifying the history,
Love of the ancestors,
Shattered.

DAWN

Dawn,
Flavoured Moon,
Tasted his sweetness,
Stars nodded head when,
Asked.

GENRE:
MICROTALE

CONTENTS

EXAM TURNDOWN

" What are you doing tonight?"

"Will Wipe off my melancholies,
Embracing scars with ecstasy,
And climb up stairs of success,
Leaving the history of failure."

Replied after her exam results.

DECISION

This shouldn't have taken place.'

' The intimacy committed between us is the result of our parallel decision .'

'You'll dump me now like others"

Unlike other:- He proposed her for marriage.

<u>DESTINATION</u>

Modernisation was the aim.

But landed up with misbehaviour. I'll practices.

Backstabbing. Disrobing respect. Dumping
parents.
Jealousy. Revenge. Same narrow thoughts.
 And an unending list of worst things.
 Vanished Humanity.

LOOK BACK

Sightseeing children playing in a park.

I thought:-
"Those were the days without any fear of
heartbreak or depression.
Was always showered with unconditional love.
With carefree mind slept peacefully.

<u>PEN</u>

Empty pen wanders over the paper with contrasting minds.

 The eager to write :

" Pens are the sword for authors ,
 to stamp the world with intricating plots to cherish and relate".

MAGIC

Mom asked : Do you believe in magic?

I replied :-
" I have the world's best parents to look after me and fulfill my desires."

Isn't this magic created by God?

TEARS

At 2 AM
 Puzzling mind convinced themselves :-
Please do not cry for the one who left us.

Heart:- They were my attachment for my eyes.

And landed up crying the loudest.

STRANGER

When he was nothing.
Heart felt he was everything.

When he became everything,
Life was nothing.

That what's his presence is - Said she.
With sparkled eyes- He smiled.

<u>STORM</u>

In the peril of night,
Being find seclusion,
For the soul who wander,
To bruise their broken pieces.
Wrapped with chaos.

- Is what is needed for a tender heart to mend.

UNCONDITIONAL

Amidst the chaos ambience,
That I can wheeze in solace.
Bounded are the thread of affection,
That coerce me to upend with gratification.

She expressed her unconditional love.

<u>HE</u>

Social media affection.
That bought two souls together .
With a random chat suddenly.

Everyone triggered with the thought of fake
online love.

They became the example to feel proud on.

LOVE RECONCEPTUALISED

He fell for him!

Society taunted the LGBT couple.

They claimed :-
"Affection is a smasher of every soul."
"Love can dwell within both the Straight and LGBT"

They redefined love!!

<u>PHRONTISTERY REMINISCNECES</u>

Going to school to study.
Going to school to meet friends.

Backbenchers made families. Played pranks.
Bunked classes. Got punishment.
-Replied a backbencher to the topper with teary
eyes.

<u>WRITING</u>

"Why do you write? "
"Writing bring nothing. "

Writing is the alcohol for aching hearts. Answer
to the imaginary minds. Words to thoughts.
Pleasure to the harsh truths.
 -Smiled an Author.

<u>AFFECTION</u>

"I love You!!"

"For?"

Exclaimed !!

"For Integrating my gremlins with a smirk,
Giving me a serendipity to amass my chimeras,
And mitigating me to chase all the pessimism
into propitiousness."

<u>GOODBYE</u>

Bleeding heart doesn't complains,
They cry their sorrow out,
When emotions tend to saturate,
They end them all in a blink.
Without an official goodbye.

-Texted my friend

- smiled in pain

<u>HATERS</u>

He sad - Now that my eyes are open!!

I can see the evils unturned,
Backstabbers hitting me hard,
Haters motivating me a lot,
Well wishers shielding me with support.

Destroyed…

TRUTH

At night she was robbed sexually when the
world was snoring.

Next day:
Society lit up candles instead of rapist.
Enquired about dress.

The rapists got courage to assault more.

<u>BOND</u>

It was the tightest hug ever.
 Tears rolled down their cheeks.
They scattered into pieces.

It was her wedding day.
It was the toughest day for both daughter and
father.

<u>ECSTASY</u>

Why are you so ecstatic? - Someone asked.

I replied-
The toxics of my life are away. The panorama of
my life is sparkling making it pulchritudinous.
Without them, I'm smiling.

AFFECTION

She was staring at him.

He asked - Why are you looking at my eyes?

She replied-
I see a zillion of stars sparkling, signifying your love for me.

They hugged.

<u>NATURAL CALAMITIES</u>

In the glowing world lies a shattered ambience which is destructed by the natural calamities. The unseen and unheard families lost their very hope of surviving.

- A victim described.

DARK

Dear Dark Time,

I have the calibre to transform you upside down.
Because positive thoughts are much more
powerful than the negative ones.
And they rule the world.

She said.

HARSH REALITY

She all dressed in red with lips glossy coloured
:- Waiting for her clients .

Society insulted her by calling prostitute.

 "Father is waiting for me at hospital for
money".-she shouted.

DREAM

Looking out my window I see birds.
Oh no!! Caged birds just like me. - Mind
Exclaimed

Calling out for help. In the havoc of the society
with curtailed dreams. -Crying

<u>SPARKLE</u>

Anniversary night :
He asked:- What do you want?

Hold me close when, I'm lamenting over my despondency, I sack out asunder. My soul gets bushwhacked. -I replied.

 Hugged in ecstasy!!

<u>PROUD</u>

"I failed "
Everyone taunted.
I cried.
"I'm proud of you. At least your tried." - Said
my father.
I laughed with pride.
He hugged me with pride. Wished me luck!! -He
smiled.

<u>PAIN</u>

Describe pain. -Someone Asked.

Ardour glides with spacious boomer cataclysmic
a mortal and shudder them with the fullest welly
either mundanely or vehemently. -I replied.

<u>CULTURE</u>

"Indian and Western culture can never coexist",
Sneered my uncle.

I smiled as I went out of the house with Hizab
and jeans.

<u>PREACHING</u>

Every sunshine is a cosmos of ecstasy.
Leaving aside the catastrophe.
Build the pillar of prosperity.
Prick your antagonist with your brighter glory"
¬-My mom taught .

Today I felt it.

GENRE: QUATRAIN & COUPLETS (RESPECTIVELY)

Men tends to be diagnosed,
With anxiety, depression, substance abuse,
antisocial disorders,
And still act as nothing is wrong with their
mental health
And subsist to be adequate for bearing
everything.

Walking on the despondent tracks,
Pondering over how messed I am,
My thoughts takes me to the roller coaster ride,
To a world with no burdens of carrying a fake
smile.

The zeal to inscribe their pieces uniquely,
Pouring all the vehemence,
No matter how simple the words seems,
But it carries a deep feeling.

The days when life wasn't camouflaged by scary
ardour,
When love was bona fide and not a subterfuge of
fornication
When lassies were free enough to stand alone at
Tenebrosity.
When the world never seem to beckon anyone.

How pulchritudinous was my infancy?
Without any trepidation of forfeiting people.
Without any scar engraved by anyone.
A phase of life where only ecstasy dwelled
leaving aside all the problems.

Love dove that I used to fear,
Has already taken me into their gear,
And has given me tear,
With a deep scar.

Amidst the chaos ambience,
That I can wheeze in solace.
Bounded are the thread of affection,
That coerce me to upend with gratification.

The night commandest to inscribe,
With pride,
Absorb the lugubrious sheet,
Spill the ecstasy.

Forgiveness is better than revenge,
But sometimes revenge is important,
To make the person suffer,
and realise the same pain.

Time heals all wounds,
Camouflaged are the feelings,
Euphoria arises again on the paths unknown,
Where once we were afraid to cross.

If the night could talk,
I would have accompanied night to walk,
Holding it tight to stalk,
Inscribing my melancholic past with chalk.

Drenching the soul the heart,
On the beach of love and affection,
Moving from the shores to the souls,
Like a couple walking from an endless route to a destiny.

While closing my eyes,
Feeling the warmth of love again,
Sighting the beauty of life,
Providing a shelter to another broken soul.

With an open heart ,
Bidding farewell to an evacuation,
With etiolating light of ecstasy,
Fighting with the self cold.

Tom and Jerry can be tagged to us,
Love and hate is imbibed within us,
Wherever you wander about,
I would be your favourite company.

Every sunshine is a cosmos of ecstasy,
Leaving aside the catastrophe,
Build the pillar of prosperity,
Prick your antagonists with your glory.

Writing the melody of the warmth and affection,
Heart singing the praises for love,
And bruishing the heart,
I tasted the sweet emotion of love and care.

Always been through the shed of share and care,
Lugubrious ambience was never my layer,
Damn went the nights,
When my tear glands flow with Vehemence.

Cool breeze brushing the soul,
And luring each other to come closer,
For a healthy romance under the open sky
staring at the stars,
Exploring the soul before touching the body.

The moon knows about,
The disaster you are facing,
Despite all the racing,
The way you are still chasing.

In the world of IPhone,
He was her Nokia,
In the world of intimation,
She was his forehead kiss.

Breaking the broken heart is easy,
Mending the broken heart is tough.

Love can dwell within anyone,
Vehemence of affection is a beauty for every
soul.

Without the fear of anything,
They render everything.

With the rotation of the earth,
The mess I'm today makes me whimper my
heart out.

On the shore of success,
Failures are the coral reefs.

Loving the pen,
Despite the pain.

Rattled oneself is battling with the thoughts,
Wanderlust is becoming the only reason to
persist.

Numbing the senses of the being to contemplate,
Spreading a lugubrious sheet over a serene
mortal.

After every perilous tenebrosity,
There comes a bright morning.

Shadowed are the paths which I crossed one day,
Hearing him has became a dream.

Friendship is not only a word but also,
Amalgamation of ecstasy and melancholy
tasting as sour and bitter.

Promises are a myth,
Playing with the feelings are a new trend.

My heart skips a beat,
When you pull me closer.

Mistakes are like an,
an integral part of everyone's life.

Struggle for a person is,
Embracement of catastrophic alley.

Bleeding hearts accepts,
The harsh reality of petrifying lanes.

A nature lover is lured by,
The beauty and charm of nature.

I feel exhausted when,
I run out if ideas to ink my dairy.

Chase your dreams,
Run behind your success.

When you try too hard not to cry,
At that phase you end up crying the loudest.

All writers have one thing in common,
The zeal to deal with their pieces uniquely.

Loving books to the core is all that I know,
Bibliophile is what I am known.

Calmness leads to utmost satisfaction,
Without any justification.

Lost souls wander about in search of peace,
Silence bruising their hearts which pours out
tears in grief.

The love stories back to 90's,
Was substantial enough to last long.

Heartiest acknowledgement
to all the readers,
From Author Naaz Nayim.

ABOUT THE PUBLICATION

Peaceful Writers International is a global Whatsapp writing community and an Indian based Publication providing Inscribing platform to amateur and budding writers to prove and brushen up their writing skills globally. It's a publication working in certain countries like

- Kenya
- Nigeria
- South Africa
- Ghana
- Zimbabwe
- Mauritius.

We provide paid publishing services, organize writing events, Open Mics, monthly fests and commemorate anthologies to celebrate the joy of writing.

Visit: www.peacefulwritersinternational.com

Or

Reach out to us:
peacefulwritersinternational@gmail.com

www.ingramcontent.com/pod-product-compliance
Lightning Source LLC
Chambersburg PA
CBHW022141150726
47992CB00002B/707